POSSIBLE WORLDS

POSSIBLE WORLDS

The Memory of Odin by Jason R. Forbus

Graphic design and layout by Sara Calmosi
Inside illustration: *Odin enthroned and holding his spear Gungnir, flanked by his ravens Huginn and Muninn and wolves Geri and Freki*, 1882, Carl Emil Doepler

Series: Possible Worlds
ISBN 979-12-5633-022-5

Ventus Press
Ali Ribelli Edizioni Group
www.aliribelli.com
redazione@aliribelli.com
Gaeta, Italy

Ventus Press, operating under the Ali Ribelli Edizioni group (Rebel Wings Publishing), is distributed worldwide through IngramSpark.

The Memory of Odin

by Jason R. Forbus

VENTUS

Gods, heroes and giants
A short essay on Norse Mythology

Norse mythology evokes images of stormy seas, snowy landscapes, enchanted forests and blood-drenched battlegrounds. Its stories tell of proud and brave warriors, dragons, trolls, dwarves and giants. The cult of Odin and Thor has greatly inspired the fantasy genre – just think of 'The Lord of the Rings' by J.R.R. Tolkien and modern role-play games.

But how did it all start?

In the beginning there was the *Ginnungagap* (literally the 'yawning void), the cosmic abyss that existed before creation.

At one point, like a sort of duplicate and parallel Big Bangs, at the respective ends of the Ginnungagap two levels of existence were formed: to the north, the frozen *Niflheimr* and to the south the unbearably hot *Múspellheimr*. Then from the center of Niflheimr 11 rivers began to flow, the Élivágar.

These rivers came so far from their source that they hardened and formed layers of frost and ice that covered Ginnungagap entirely. But the warm winds of Múspellheimr melted the ice, and from the drops that followed the first beings of the cosmos formed: *Ymir*, father of the Frost Giants, and *Auðhumla*, the 'cosmic cow' whose milk fed the infant Ymir to a sturdy and godly adulthood.

> Of old was the age when Ymir lived;
> Sea nor cool waves nor sand there were;
> Earth had not been, nor heaven above,
> But a yawning gap, and grass nowhere.

Poetic Edda *Völuspá*, third stanza

Ymir was a wise, but evil being, as all his descendants after him would be. As he stared into the great, lonely void all around him, he resolved not to waste his energies and decided to take a long nap instead. He curled up for the night and soon began to sweat copiously. Each drop of his sweat turned into a giant, and thus that warring race was begotten. But his innate power to create life did not stop there: under his left arm, a man and a woman were born while from his legs came a son with six heads, with the unpronounceable name of Þrúðgelmir.

While Ymir slept, the cosmic cow did not stay idle. You can imagine at that time food was in really short supply, so t the wretched animal had to resort to licking salt that crusted some icy stones. As she licked, on the very first day, towards evening, she brought to light a hair of a man; the following day his head and on the third day the whole person. The man was called *Búri* ('the producer'), who generated a son identical to himself who was called *Borr* ('the begotten' – and by the way, food wasn't the only thing in short supply in those days).

Borr went on to marry *Bestla* (granddaughter of the frost giant *Bölþorn*, and what a terrible father-in-law he must have been!) and he had three children with her. The first was named *Odin*, the second *Vili* and the third *Vé*.

One day, just as had happened with *Kronos* and his children the Olympians, the three gods decided to kill Ymir and to drown in his blood all the giants that he had generated. The sole survivors were *Bergelmir*, son of the six-headed Þrúðgelmir, and his bride. It is from them that the lineage of Frost Giants would continue.

Following this heinous act, and not knowing how to get rid of the exceedingly cumbersome corpse of Ymir, Odin and his brothers decided to use it to create *Midgard* (or 'Middle-earth', ring a bell?), right smack in the middle of the Ginnungagap. Ymir's eyebrows became the planet itself, a sort of shelter from the fury of the giants. Instead, Ymir's flesh became earth, his blood lakes and rivers, his bones mountains, his teeth and the remains of his bones stones, while from his hair grew the trees.

The birth of the dwarves is certainly not as fancy as you would expect: our bearded friends originated from the larvae feasting on the putrid corpse of Ymir (Yuk!). Not fully satisfied with the level of eeriness of their art work, the gods placed Ymir's skull above the Ginnungagap and thus created the heavenly vault, supported by four dwarfs (hope they get some days off every now and then). Their names were: *Norðri, Suðri, Austri* and *Vestri*, and just so you know the cardinal points are named after them.

Odin then placed one of Bergelmir's sons, the shape-shifter *Hræsvelgr*, at the end of the earth. The giant transformed into a giant eagle, and began to powerfully flap its wings, generating the wind that crosses the world in all directions.

With the bones taken care of, the gods went on and pulled poor *Ymir*'s brain out and broke it into several pieces these they tossed in the air like confetti that transformed into puffy clouds (think about that the next time you are lying on the grass looking at the heavens and marveling at the clouds).

Lastly, they collected the sparks from Muspellheimr and spread them all across the Ginnungagap, creating the light and the stars.

Norse cosmology is comprised of 9 worlds (*Nío Heimar* in Old Norse). Except *Midgard*, which roughly corresponds to Scandinavia, the remaining eight worlds can be divided into pairs of opposites: the aforementioned Múspellheimr and Niflheimr, fire and heat vs ice and cold; *Asaheimr* and *Hel*, which can loosely be interpreted as Christian Heaven and Hell; *Vanaheimr* and *Jötunheimr*, creation and destruction; *Alfheimr* and *Svartálfaheimr*, light and darkness.

All these worlds are connected to each other by the Tree of the World, *Yggdrasill.*

An ash I know there stands,
Yggdrasill is its name,
a tall tree, showered
with shining loam.
From there come the dews
that drop in the valleys.
It stands forever green over
Urðr's well.

Poetic Edda *Völuspá*, second stanza

According to the most widely accepted interpretation of the myths, the branches of *Yggdrasill* would extend far into the heavens, while the tree would be supported by three roots that extend far away into other locations; one to the well *Urðarbrunnr* in the heavens, one to the spring *Hvergelmir*, and another to the well *Mímisbrunnr*. The importance of *Yggdrasill* in Norse Cosmology is further highlighted in the Poetic Edda Völuspá, the 'Prophecy of the *Völva*' ('Seeress' in Old Norse):

I remember nine worlds,
nine in the tree,
the great measuring-tree,
down in the mould.

But what about the gods and supernatural creatures that populate Norse mythology? The deities are divided in two classes: the Æsir and the *Vanir*, the latter less known and somehow subordinate to the former. The distinction, however, is not clear: in the distant past the two factions faced each other in war but later agreed to peace, exchanged hostages and even joined in marriage. Moreover, membership to one of the two classes is not crystal clear for some deities.

One thing that Æsir and Vanir have in common is their general hatred of the *Jötnar* (singular *Jötunn*). The *Jötnar* are a type of entity contrasted with gods and other figures, such as dwarves and elves. The entities are themselves ambiguously defined and variously referred to by several other terms, including *troll*. Trolls may be ugly and slow-witted, or look and behave exactly like human beings, with no particularly grotesque characteristics about them.

Generally speaking, the Jötnar are not necessarily notably large and their features range from great beauty to astonishing grotesqueness. It should also be noted that both the Æsir and the *Vanir* can join with Jötnar to generate children, when the latter are not monsters. Indeed, some deities such as *Skaði* and *Gerðr*, are themselves described as Jötnar, and various well-known deities, such as Odin, are descendants of the Jötnar.

As for the giants, here too we are presented with two general classes: the *Hrímþursar*, the 'giants of hoarfrost', and the Múspellsmegir or 'fire giants' also called 'Sons of Muspell'. Whether you like your tea cool or hot, giants are presented as element-based creatures, and should therefore not be confused with trolls. In fact, while giants tend to live in clans and take an active role in Norse Mythology, especially in regards to their interaction with gods and humans, trolls tend to live in isolatation and avoid any involvement in the affairs of humans and divine beings alike.

Other well-known supernatural beings are *Fenrir* the wolf and *Miðgarðsormr*, the great serpent that surrounds the world of Midgard. Both are the children that the trickster god *Loki* had with a giantess. Other creatures often mentioned are *Huginn* and *Muninn*, respectively 'thought' and 'memory', the two ravens that keep Odin informed about everything that happens in the Nine Worlds. *Sleipnir*, Odin's eight-legged horse, is also a son of *Loki* (the art of lying makes him a true *Casanova* with the ladies).

Ratatosk instead is the annoying and, it can be safely assumed, insane squirrel that runs up and down Yggdrasill, the Tree of the World, to deliver insults to the dragon *Níðhöggr* (anglicized *Nidhogg*, the 'Malice Striker'… you better stay away from this one!) from an unnamed eagle:

There is much to be told. An eagle sits at the top of the ash, and it has knowledge of many things. Between its eyes sits the hawk called *Vedrfolnir* […]. The squirrel called Ratatosk runs up and down the ash. He tells slanderous gossip, provoking the eagle and Nidhogg.

Prose Edda book *Gylfaginning*

And, in the Poetic Edda poem *Grímnismál:*

> Ratatosk is the squirrel who there shall run
> On the ash-tree Yggdrasil;
> From above the words of the eagle he bears,
> And tells them to Nithhogg beneath.

We should also mention the possible presence atop of *Yggdrasil* of another being, *Víðópnir* the golden rooster. According to the *Fjölsvinnsmál*, the second of two Old Norse poems commonly published under the title *Svipdagsmál* ('The Lay of *Svipdagr*'), *Víðópnir* is a rooster that sits at the top of *Mímameiðr*, a tree often taken to be identical to the World Tree Yggdrasil. According to the myth, it will be Víðópnir who will announce the beginning of *Ragnarok*.

However, the creature inhabiting Yggdrasil that is of worthiest note is certainly the dragon Niddhog, a horrid monster whose scales are littered with the remains of the unlucky warriors who tried their fortune against him. The dragon's favourite hobby is to eternally gnaw at the roots of the World Tree, a relentless activity that will eventually cause its catastrophic fall. As described in the poem Grímnismál:

> A hall I saw,
> far from the sun,
> On Nastrond it stands,

and the doors face north,
Venom drops
through the smoke-vents down,
For around the walls
do serpents wind.
I there saw wading
through rivers wild
treacherous men
and murderers too,
And workers of ill
with the wives of men;
There Nithhogg sucked
the blood of the slain,
And the wolf tore men;
would you know yet more?

The unlucky tree must also endure the hunger of the four stags, *Dáinn, Dvalinn, Duneyrr* and *Duraþrór*, who carelessly chomp at its branches.

But let us leave Yggdrasil and its inhabitants and take a more general look at Norse Mythology.

As with other polytheistic religions, Norse mythology presents a weak opposition between Good and Evil, which is instead typical of monotheistic traditions. *Loki*, for example, the principle and prince of disorder, on many occasions assists his fellow gods with his cunning, and in many others he insults them and causes them grief. Giants are also not fundamentally evil but rude, boastful and uncivilized. The contrast here is between the principles of Order and Chaos, eternally battling each other and the balance of the cosmos shifting one way and another.

In this light, the infamous *Ragnarök* (the 'Fate of the Gods') is the final act of Chaos that in its might floods all of the Nine Worlds, bringing an end to the Norse way of understanding the universe. The sources describing Ragnarök, like almost all of those on Norse mythology, are fragmentary, confusing, contradictory, filled with cryptic references and often incomprehensible in their laconism.

According to the texts that survive to our day, Ragnarök will be preceded by the *Fimbulvetr,* a terrible winter lasting three years, perhaps a reminiscence of the Ice Age? Just as in the case of the Great Flood, which is recounted in many religious traditions, the Fimbulvetr too might have at its origins a true event or period of the world. In any case, following this three-year winter all social and family ties will break down in an unstoppable vortex of violence.

Then the Sun and the Moon will disappear: *Sköll and Hati,* the wolves who pursued the two celestial bodies since the beginning of time, will at last devour them, thus depriving the world of all natural light. Even the stars will go out like candles in the wind.

Deep underground, Nidhogg will sever the last root of the World Tree, causing Yggdrasill to shake and in its tumult dissolve all the boundaries separating the Nine Worlds.

This will cause earthquakes, floods and natural disasters of immense proportion.

It is then that the creatures of chaos will launch their assault: Fenrir the wolf will be freed from its chains, while Miðgarðsormr the sea-serpent will emerge from the depths of the waters. The infernal ship *Naglfar* will set its tattered sail and carry the Champions of Chaos to battle, and at its helm will be the giant *Hrymr*.

For their part, the mysterious Múspellsmegir, the Fire Giants, will not remain idle and in their blazing fury they will ride on *Bifröst*, the burning 'Rainbow Bridge' that extends between *Midgard* and *Asgard* (the realm of the gods), causing it to collapse. At this point *Heimdallr*, the white guardian god, will blow into his horn, the *Gjallarhorn*, to summon the gods and the warriors of *Valhalla* to the final battle between Order and Chaos.

In the great final combat each deity will clash with his nemesis, in mutual destruction. The wolf Fenrir will devour Odin, who will then be avenged by his son *Viðarr*.

[...]
and there the son proclaims on his horse's back
that he's keen to avenge his father."

Grímnismál, stanza 17

This latter and relatively obscure deity is referred to in Norse mythology as 'the silent god'; he is supposedly nearly as strong as the god *Thor*, and gods rely on him in times of immense difficulties.

Pop-culture favorite *Thor* and the serpent *Miðgarðsormr* will slay each other in combat, and the same fate will befall *Týr* and the infernal hound *Garmr* (*Cerberus,* English-world *Hellhounds,* Catalonia's *Dip*, etc., - in ancient myths, human's best friend often turn into their worst enemy), and Heimdallr and Loki.

At last, the powerful *Surtr* ('black' or 'the swarthy one') will cut down the great god *Freyr*, who is associated with sacred kingship, virility and prosperity, and set the world on fire with his flaming sword.

Therefore, Norse mythology's *Armageddon* starts with ice – the three-year Fimbulvetr – but ends in fire.

From the ashes, as a post-Deluge awakening, the world will rise again. The sons of Odin, *Víðarr* and Váli, and the sons of Thor, *Móði* and *Magni*, will inherit the powers of their fathers. *Baldr*, the god of hope and *Höðr* his brother will return from *Hel*, the realm of death. They will find, in the grass of the new meadows, the chess pieces with which the vanquished gods once played (this is likely a medieval addition to the original myth).

And what about us humans?

The human race will be regenerated by a new original couple, blond-haired 'Adam and Eve', respectively *Líf* and *Lífþrasir*, who will survive the *Ragnarök* by hiding in the *Hoddmímir* forest.

The rebirth of the world, however, is overshadowed by

the flight, high in the sky, of Níðhöggr the dragon (a bad penny always turns up, or so they say).

What is most surprising about Norse mythology is precisely this 'fate of the gods', which fascinates us for its ineluctability and for the courage shown by its protagonists even in the face of death. The same principle that, together with abundant libations of beer and mead, drove the notorious *berserkers* towards likely death or maiming in battle in a not-so-distant past and, from there, a one-way ticket to coveted *Valhalla*, the 'Hall of the Slain':

"What kind of a dream is it," said *Óðinn*,
in which just before daybreak,
I thought I cleared *Valhǫll*,
for the coming of slain men?
I woke the *Einherjar*,
bade the *valkyries* rise up,
to strew the bench,
and scour the beakers,
wine to carry,
as for a king's coming,
here to me I expect
heroes' coming from the world,
certain great ones,
so glad is my heart.

Chapter 8 of *Fagrskinna*

Bibliography

Bellows, Henry A. (1936) translation. *The Poetic Edda.* Princeton University Press

Byock, Jesse (Trans.) (2006). *The Prose Edda. Penguin Classics.* ISBN 0-14-044755-5

Faulkes, Anthony (Trans.) (1995). Edda. Everyman. ISBN 0-460-87616-3

Finlay, Alison (2004). *Fagrskinna, a Catalogue of the Kings of Norway: A Translation with Introduction and Notes.* Brill Publishers. ISBN 90-04-13172-8

Hollander, M. Lee (Trans.) (2007). *Heimskringla: History of the Kings of Norway.* University of Texas Press. ISBN 978-0-292-73061-8

Larrington, Carolyne (Trans.) (1999). *The Poetic Edda. Oxford World's Classics.* ISBN 0-19-283946-2

Orchard, Andy (1997). *Dictionary of Norse Myth and Legend.* Cassell. ISBN 0-304-34520-2

Orel, Vladimir (2003). *A Handbook of Germanic Etymology.* Brill. ISBN 9004128751

Simek, Rudolf (2007) translated by Angela Hall. *Dictionary of Northern Mythology.* D.S. Brewer ISBN 0-85991-513-1

Viktor Rydberg (1886). *Gods and Goddesses of the Northland,* The Norrœna Society

Watkins, Calvert (2000). *The American Heritage Dictionary of Indo-European Roots.* Houghton Mifflin Company. IBSN 0-395-98610-9

GESTUMBLINDI said:

"Who is the great one that glides o'er the earth,
and swallows both waters and woods?
The wind he fears, but weights nowise,
and seeks to harm the sun.
Aright guess now this riddle, Heithrek!"

HEITHREK said:

"Good is thy riddle, Gestumblindi,
and guessed it is:
That is the fog. One cannot see the sun because of him,
but he disappears when the wind blows, and men can do
naught against him. He kills the light of the sun."

From 'The Riddles of King Heithrek', *Heithreksgátur*

The Memory of Odin

So it is said in the Poetic Edda *Grímnismál*, XX stanza:

> "Huginn ok Munin
> fljúga hverjan dag
> Jörmungrund yfir;
> óumc ek of Hugin
> at hann aftr né comiþ,
> þó siámc meir um
> Munin."

> "Hugin and Munin
> fly each day
> over the spacious earth.
> I fear for Hugin,
> that he come not back,
> yet more anxious am I for
> Munin."

It was the dawn of an icy morning in Midgard. The tall mountains, the deep fjords and the immense forests, all were shrouded in fog and buried in snow, fast asleep under an expanse of suffocating whiteness. No man or animal could be seen. None, that is, besides a small black dot daring the frigid sky, a raven flying between storm-filled clouds and towering mountains.

The wings of the raven were numb with cold and fatigue, yet he stubbornly flew onwards against the howling wind, calling amid the rocky walls of the mountains: "Muninn! Muninn!", but his calls went unheeded, his cries lost like an echo in a crevasse.

The raven flew for hours without pause, keeping steady in his flight until his strength abandoned him. Then, as the grey day grew darker, he looked for shelter. Despite the snowflakes madly swirling all around him, he was able to spot a cavity in the rock, and there he roughly glided. It was a dark and inhospitable place, an ice cave where no man had ever set foot. The raven perched as best he could, curling up to retain what little heat remained in his frail body.

"I mustn't close my eyes" he told himself, "or I will freeze and remain in this cave until the end of days". He couldn't help but think that Muninn might have suffered the same terrible fate. Perhaps his friend, overcome by hunger and fatigue, had finally sought refuge in a cave and once there he had found the bittersweet consolation of death.

Huginn tried to dispel those grim thoughts with logical thinking: "If this is what's happened, then He would have known it". But would he really? Since Muninn's disappearance, their Lord had changed: he seemed older than he really was, and tired, weary as a mountain that has borne the ages of the world on its rocky back and is finally about to collapse. Their Lord had begun to forget things he should not and could not forget. Maybe Muninn really had died, alone and desperate, in a dark cave in the mountains…

"I mustn't close my eyes, I must not…" but his weariness was too great to endure and with sadness weighing heavy in his heart, the raven closed his eyes, finally defeated by the deadly embrace of oblivion.

***

Despite being large and almost as tall as the cave, he barely made any noise as he advanced on the ice floor one stealthy step at a time. The roaring wind outside swept away all noise, and before long his large hairy hands locked onto the unsuspecting bird. He held the raven as gently as he could, but to poor little Huginn that grip was as painful and horrid as the clutch of death.

Awoken and half in shock, the raven for a moment thought a big chunk of ice had fallen from the ceiling and crashed to the ground near him. Only later, with his head poking out of the cupped fist of his abductor, did he realize he'd become the unfortunate prey of a Frost Giant.

"I have you!" The giant shouted triumphantly, swinging the raven around as if he were a trophy.

"Ouch! Let me go, craaa!" Huginn's loud protest caused the giant's big blue eyes to grow larger still.

"You… speak?" and he stared at him as a child first looks at fire. Frightened and in pain, Huginn thought quickly about a way to get out of his predicament.

"Yes, I can speak. Truly, I am a sorcerer wandering the Earth in disguise. Release me immediately, and I will let you go unscathed."

The threat seemed to have a certain effect on the giant, who stared at him for a few seconds, until a toothy smile spread over his pallid face.

"What a funny little bird you are. You enter my house without being invited, and dare threaten me".

"Let me go, I say, if you hold your life dear!" Huginn insisted, this time though with a hint of fear in his croaks.

"No, I won't let you go. I've grown sick and tired of filling my belly with ice and rocks. They don't taste like much and cause me to sleep badly. You're a scrawny little thing, but better than rocks for sure. Hope you don't mind if I take a bite!" and with a horrible and cavernous laughter he brought the raven close to his mouth. Huginn closed his eyes and braced for the worst, but just then a loud and shrill voice boomed from deep inside the cavern: "Stop, Gümrad!"

Slowly, Huginn opened his eyes to see a very tall and muscular woman, powerful and yet graceful, coming towards them with determined steps. It was a *gýgr*, a giantess. She was clothed in heavy white bear fur and her soft white hair reminded him of fresh snow.

"What kind of husband are you?! Did you want to eat it without telling me?" She shouted and put her foot down to show her stern disapproval. The giant, probably used to her sudden outbursts, simply rolled his eyes and let out a deep sigh.

"Gýgr! You are always complaining! I found it, and I'm going to eat it!" But the giantess wasn't going to give up that succulent snack so easily.

"I too am tired of filling my stomach with ice and stone! No animal, nor soft little human to eat for days… Listen to my words: if you eat that raven, indigestion will suck away what little brain you have left and then what good will it have done to you?" then, suddenly softening like the calm after the storm, "Come on, Gümrad son of Wümrad, if we do not help each other, we will not survive the Fimbulwinter…".

But Gümrad son of Wümrad was firm in his decision and, like a stubborn child:

"I said no. I found it and I'm going to eat it!"

He reopened his jaws and this time narrowly missed biting off Huginn's head with his horribly sharp teeth. But the giantess wasn't going to let that happen. With the agility of a tiger, she suddenly leaped at him, her eyes blind with fury.

"My sisters warned me not to marry you!" she shouted in his face while with nails and bites she tried to steal from him that thin and coveted meal.

Gümrad's dim brain took a few seconds to realize what had happened. In the meanderings of his mind, usually dark and silent as the beginnings of universe, a spark ignited and quickly grew until it burst into a shout so loud and so full of anger that the walls of the cave shook wildly, causing ancient stalactites of ice to crash to the floor.

A moment later, husband and wife were locked together in mortal combat. Against the brute force of the giant, the giantess showed surprising agility. There was very little conjugal spirit in that bloody brawl; kicks and punches followed one after another with the purpose of annihilating the opponent. A minute into the fight the two lost their balance, but just before they hit the ground Huginn managed to free himself from the giant's grip and escape. Flying out of the cave the raven turned to take a last look inside: the giants, now completely forgetful of him, carried on their fierce struggle.

"I can't believe I made it out alive!" Huginn reflected, congratulating his good fortune and blessing the quick temper of the giants.

But outside the cave the blizzard raged on. He sought another shelter but the snow fell so thickly and the wind was so strong that the raven flew blindly in the night.

He struggled for a few more minutes until the last of his

strength, his last drop of warm blood and last dry feather. Then a whirlwind seized him and darkness descended on the world.

***

It had been years since he had smelled the fresh scent of grass or flowers. He also felt a sudden warmth flood his cold bones. Was he dead?

"Come and take a look, Lif! It woke up!"

At first unsure what he was experiencing, once his eyes were open he saw a pretty girl come into view, looking at him with joyful eyes. She had copper-red hair and a beautiful smile.

The boy named Lif came forward. He was a few years older than the girl, and his face was noble and good. He leaned over the small wooden cage and looked at Huginn carefully, before allowing himself a smile.

"He will recover soon. You did well, Lifthrasir. But let him rest a little more before freeing him. He is still very weak".

The girl nodded. Then, like a child stealing candy, she slipped her fingers into the cage and stroked Huginn softly. After the giant's steel grip, the gentle touch of those tapered fingers was a caress from heaven.

Huginn looked around: he would have sworn that he was in the middle of a large pine and fir forest. At one time he would certainly not have marveled at the sight of such a familiar landscape, but that was the third and last year of the Fimbulwinter, the long winter without spring that had covered the whole world of Midgard under an unforgiving blanket of snow and ice. In that place, however, everything was lush and the Sun shone beyond the thick leaves of the trees, piercing the undergrowth with a dense web of rays. But the greatest mystery came from the two children who, despite the full beauty of their young age, were dressed poorly and looked malnourished.

Huginn tried to remember what had happened, but his last memory before losing consciousness was falling, exhausted, into the void. On awakening, he'd found himself in that green forest and under the loving care of those children…but how many days had passed? His Lord must be worried about him. Perhaps, at that moment, he was scanning the horizon, tormenting himself: "So Huginn too has abandoned me".

The raven quickly thought about what to do. He could wait until the children let him go. After all, a little rest would do him good. Still, he felt his time was running out and that he should better hurry.

Ordering "Release me or my wrath will fall upon you!" was obviously a bad idea: slender as she was, the girl would faint or flee, making him lose precious time. Huginn tried to remember an opening spell but none came to his mind. After some hesitation, he finally decided to opt for what seemed to be the best choice.

"Thank you, kind maiden, for your loving care".

What had he been thinking? The girl's reaction was more than predictable. She let out a cry and quickly withdrew her hand from the cage. The boy instantly appeared at her side.

"What is it, Lifthrasir? Did you see them?" he said as he gently took her hand.

"N-no Lif, It's not them, but… the raven! The raven spoke to me!"

"By Thor's hammer, what foolishness is this? You gave me quite a scare, you know. To think that a raven can talk… You must be tired, maybe it's better if you get some rest".

"In this case," Huginn interjected, "I would recommend that you also take a nap."

Lif's eyes widened in amazement, not quite sure whether what he had heard was real or the fruit of his imagination. Still he stood before Lifthrasir, and after a better scrutiny confronted the raven.

"What kind of spell is this? Are you a wizard?"

"Do not fear, I do not mean you any harm. I only want you to free me so that I can continue my journey. But first tell me, what place is this, where everything is green and the Sun is shining?"

"You are in Hodmimir's wood, talking raven – but I'm pretty sure you knew this already" – the boy's handsome face became serious and his forehead wrinkled in concern – "I won't trust you: you could be one of them in disguise…"

Huginn cursed his damned tongue. Didn't Muninn always tell him that he talked too much?

"Do you really believe he is a spy?"

"I don't even know who you're talking about and neither do I care. I ended up in this place by chance and now my duty calls me elsewhere. Let me go, please!"

The girl looked at Huginn with sympathy, but Lif was resolute.

"Remember, Lifthrasir, how they deceived your father and the warriors of the village? They said they were travelers and they believed them. But that night, while the village was asleep, the guests thanked us with torches and steel!"

"You are right, Lif…"

The girl looked down, perhaps in an attempt to escape the glare of the flames that still burned in her memory. Still in her heart she could not believe that this small and defenseless animal meant any harm. She was torn in two by doubt and eventually decided to rely on Lif's firmness.

Things looked bad for Huginn. Every second was precious. If his saviors, now his jailers, did not decide to free him, the already-small chance he had of finding Muninn would be reduced practically to zero. Huginn was about to reply when, suddenly, there was the gloomy and threatening thunder of a horn. A strange silence followed that ominous call. The creatures of the forest seemed to have vanished, perhaps presaging a disaster.

"They are here, they have come!" the boy barely whispered. He fell silent. From the black depths of the forest came terror.

From the way they howled, Huginn would have sworn that they were wolves. But no Midgard wolf barked in the language of men. The raven concluded that these creatures were not human beings, but to which degenerate race they belonged he could not say.

Regaining his courage, Lif grabbed a stick and courageously prepared for the worst.

"Let the berserkers[1] be cursed! They will pay dearly for their destruction of Lerwik!".

But, as he spoke, his hands trembled like leaves, those hands that had seen too few winters.

"Let's try to escape to the mountain!" suggested Lifthrasir, pulling on his shirt sleeve.

"It would be useless. They're too fast for us and still have a better sense of smell than the beasts. We cannot do anything but face them and die with honor."

The girl said nothing, letting silence speak for her. In her eyes that remembered spring, Huginn did not see fear. The raven immediately recognized that look, as he had seen it countless times before, near the roaring sea. It was in that

---

[1] Fierce Scandinavian warriors traditionally loyal to the god Odin. Before battle, they entered a state of fury called "berserksgangr" that made them particularly ferocious and insensitive to pain.

way, with those same absent eyes that the handmaidens had followed their sire on his last journey, contemplating the flames lapping at the hull of the *drakkar*,[2] consuming the corpse of the king and all that belonged to him in life, including their young lives offered in sacrifice. It was a look full of anguish and forgetfulness, the resignation of those who continue to breathe but live no more.

The berserkers, those half-man and half-beast creatures, were now very close. The raven felt pity for those children, whose young lives seemed destined to be broken by cruel blades. Besides, there was nothing he could do to save them. In spite of his poor memory, he remembered perfectly the warning of his Lord: "You must not be interested in the affairs of mortal beings. If you prefer, look at them as you would observe a stone. Would you help a landslide of stone, Huginn?"

For many years Huginn had respected those orders. He knew that behind those words there was great wisdom. If mortals had entrusted their fortunes and misfortunes to the will of the gods, the world of Midgard would have become a mere shadow of Asgard. A shadow that neither gods nor mortals desired.

---

[2] The drakkar was a boat used mainly by Vikings and Saxons for military purposes during the Middle Ages, and for exploratory trips to Iceland and Greenland.

However, observing the trembling hands of Lif and the eyes of Lifthrasir staring with resignation at the ground, those orders that he once had believed wise seemed now to be cruel.

He was immersed in these thoughts when the first berserker emerged from the thick trees. He wore a heavy bear skin over rippling muscles and brandished a blood-encrusted ax. The warrior looked at the unhappy children fiercely and then, grinding his yellow teeth in a terrifying grimace, yelled; it was the cry of a madman, of a blood-thirsty demon with an ax in his hands. Leaping, the figure of the berserker took on a mystical connotation, like the avatar of a mighty god of carnage. Shortly thereafter, his heavy ax would have fallen on the children, crushing them. Faced with such horror, Lif closed his eyes. It was too much for him too. When, suddenly…

"Stop!" the raven croaked with all the breath he had.

When the blow did not come, the boy opened his eyes and this time he remained frozen with fear. Just one meter from him, his face transformed into an animal grimace, there was the berserker who, sweaty and panting, seemed about to strike the fatal blow, but for some mysterious reason was holding back. He stood still and looked at him with a blank stare. A second later he lowered his ax. The bloodthirsty and furious warrior of a moment before had vanished and, in his place, an idiot had appeared. Lif breathed a sigh of relief, the best – he thought – of his entire life.

"Now turn around."

There could be no doubt: the command had come from the mysterious talking raven. What would happen now? Lif's relief was eclipsed by new fears: what if the raven really was an evil wizard? He could only pray to all the gods in Asgard that the bird had good intentions.

Another order from the raven forced the berserker to move away, disappearing into the woods. Lif could hardly believe that the ferocious beast had been tamed with simple words from a small raven! But it was too early to declare victory; suddenly, from the thick of the trees, a roar of shouts exploded and a moment later, as if evoked by thunder, four other berserkers appeared in the clearing. They also wore thick bear fur stained with dried blood, and wielded weapons that could have cut down a tree with one blow. Their hideous faces, marked by many scars, told of innumerable massacres.

The two children were surrounded in less than a moment. The youngsters must have amused and excited those brutes, who began to rant against the children in an incomprehensible dialect, even going so far as to lick with sinister mockery their blades encrusted with blood. Lif and Lifthrasir stood motionless, stunned by that horrible spectacle. Suddenly one of the Berserkers, the biggest and most ferocious one, pounced on them, pointing his long and heavy sword. But the berserker did not have time to move more than one step when from behind him an unexpected and lethal blow from an ax split his skull in two. A gush of dark blood spurted from the mutilated body, spraying the stunned faces of the other warriors. Their eyes immediately turned to the warrior who had launched that deadly blow, the same one that the raven had bewitched a few minutes before and who, taking advantage of the distraction of his companions, had snuck up on them. Their confused reaction lasted a moment too long: again the ax struck, cutting off the arm of another warrior. The scream of pain echoed through the silent wood. And so the orgy of blood began.

After their initial amazement wore off, the berserkers attacked their comrade, but a moment later, victims of their own blood frenzy, they started striking blindly, hitting each other indiscriminately. In just a few seconds, all the fighters lay dead or dying on the ground. The clearing was now reduced to a pool of blood, splinters of steel and human remains. Lif asked Lifthrasir to move away. A death rattle was heard, then silence once again reigned in the Wood of Hodmimir.

Upon reaching Lifthrasir, the boy bent to the ground and observed the raven closely. He then asked, "How did you do that?".

Huginn was exhausted, it was an effort to respond. When was the last time he had dominated a creature's mind? He was sure that at least two centuries had passed. His magical arts had long remained dormant, perhaps too long, tucked away in favor of the arts of diplomacy and subterfuge.

He had forgotten many incantations, but perhaps being cornered had reminded him.

"I dominated… his mind… now do you believe me?"

"Of course we believe you! Isn't that true, Lif?" said the girl, looking intently at the boy.

"Can you ever forgive my suspicions, talking raven?" The boy tried to justify himself, "we live in difficult times and you can imagine that it's not easy, you know…to trust a creature like you".

"I forgive you, boy. But now, what do you say, free me from this cage, hmm? I desperately need to stretch my wings and resume my journey".

The boy opened the cage a little hesitantly. What else could this strange talking raven, this sorcerer do? But seeing the raven hop out on unsteady legs and happily flap his wings reassured him.

"Free at last! Come on, let's leave this place and find another shelter. While I regain my strength, I want you to tell me your whole story. Why are you here? And above all, *where is here?*"

The walk from the bloodstained clearing to the new shelter, located along the banks of a cool and lively stream, perhaps gave the young people time to put their memories in order, for they had just begun to dip their legs into the water before, without the raven's encouragement, resuming their story.

"Those berserkers you defeated" began Lif clenching his fists, "they have denied Odin and sworn loyalty to Loki. Judging by their monstrous appearance, I would readily swear that they are a cross between humans and giants. These monsters roam the earth in small bands, burning and destroying everything they encounter on their way".

"It is said that in return for their help and as a reward for their loyalty, Loki has promised them the world of Midgard when the Ragnarök ends".

"Fools! Loki never keeps his word. They will pay the great Odin dearly for their treachery" interrupted Huginn, who just could not keep his thoughts to himself.

"I imagined. His own servants are the lowest traitors! Some time ago, five of them came to our village. They swore that they were simple travelers looking for shelter for the night. But their appearance worried us, and no one had visited the village in months, ever since the news of trouble in the mountains.

"The father of Lifthrasir, who was the head of the village, called an assembly to decide what to do, as is always done on these occasions. Some spell had in the meantime clouded the minds of our warriors, as none of them seemed to notice the foreigner's grim appearance. They said letting them die in the cold right outside the gates of our village would have been cruel. Well, the gods punished our insane act of mercy. That same night, when the last torches went out, the strangers crawled out of their beds and opened the gates to the rest of their band...

"When the first fires were set, the whole village woke up: men, women and children took up swords and sticks and hurled themselves at the attackers. It was then that the berserkers showed themselves for what they really were, heartless and bloodthirsty monsters. We defended ourselves with all our strength, fighting to the last. We killed many of those bastards but they were too many. The battle was lost from the start. Those bandits spared no one!

"It was the end of the world, at least the world I knew. I wandered about in that red-hot chaos, ready to sacrifice my life in battle to join my ancestors in Valhalla, when I saw her…at first, blinded by the smoke of the fires and the blood that dripped into my eyes, I mistook her for a Valkyrie. But no, it was Lifthrasir, little Lifthrasir who stumbled aimlessly through that landscape of death and ruin. It was then that I made my decision…" he smiled at her.

"Yes. I… I don't remember much of what happened after the attack. I seemed to be walking in a nightmare of fire, steel and screams. I remember that Lif scolded me" the girl's cheeks flushed crimson, "he told me 'come away from there, silly!', isn't that true, Lif? And then I felt your hands grabbing me and suddenly I stopped dreaming. What I remember later is the rush to escape the smoking ruins, the screaming people …"

A river of tears at this point prevented her from continuing. No matter how much she tried to deny it to herself and the others, the horror of that terrible night had followed her to the Wood of Hodmimir, and all the caresses and blandishments of Midgard would not return to her that wonderful smile. Perhaps, Huginn thought, that night Lif had not been wrong, he may have really seen a Valkyrie: a part of Lifthrasir that followed the dead on their last journey…

"After escaping from the village", the boy resumed, "we wandered aimlessly for days, in a desolate and hopeless landscape. We traveled day and night, with cold and hunger as companions. The fear of the berserkers haunted us even when we hid ourselves in caves to find sleep. We were startled by the slightest noise. In those days we ate anything we could find…even carrion. Wildlife out there, as you have seen for yourself, is scarce indeed. I fear that all the animals are dead, victims to the cold and the supernatural beasts that roam the lands.

"We too would have suffered that sad fate. Perhaps, I thought in those days, it would have been better to have died in Lerwik along with my people, earning Valhalla heroically; perhaps my ancestors had cursed me to wander forever for those frozen lands…so, extremely weak and almost frozen, there remained little hope for us, when…"

Suddenly his eyes widened, interrupting the story.

"…when? Go on boy, speak up".

"A raven, Lif! Remember?"

"A raven?"

Huginn's curiosity instantly lit up.

"Yes! You should know that when everything seemed lost, over our heads we saw a raven fly. We had not seen other living creatures for days, so we decided to follow the direction it flew in. After a day and a half of walking and with a little luck, to our surprise, we came to this green valley. For some inexplicable reason, as you can see for yourself, these woods have remained untouched by the fury of winter…

"Indeed, other people had arrived before us. They also told us they had arrived in the valley following the flight of that mysterious raven. An elder who knew the ancient stories claimed that this must be the legendary Wood of Hodmimir, the evergreen forest, and we attributed our arrival to divine intervention and we stopped thinking about the raven or worrying about the long winter which undoubtedly raged beyond the valley. Everything went well for a while. We were beginning to build a new life until, one sad day, we heard the sinister call of horns resounding in the woods. Lifthrasir and I immediately recognized that hateful sound. The nightmare was not over yet: the berserkers had discovered Hodmimir!

"In a few days, this beautiful and serene place turned into a battlefield. Once again we fought to the best of our ability, inflicting heavy losses among the ranks of the berserkers. But the fighting destroyed both parties. In all likelihood, the berserkers that you defeated were the last of their group and, I fear, Lifthrasir and I are the last inhabitants of Hodmimir …"

"And what can you tell me about the raven? Did any of you see him again?"

"Old Arvid swore he saw it fly towards the east" the boy pointed to a spot where the woods broke against a high rock face, "but in those days we did not take too much notice".

Now that he had a direction, however hypothetical, Huginn could linger no more. Tired or not, he had to get back into the air immediately and resume his search.

"I think it's time for me to go…"

The boy wanted to ask the talking raven many things before it left; an explanation of all these mysteries, the berserkers, the long winter that had scourged the outside world, the enchanted forest, talking ravens and sorcerers. But it was Lifthrasir who asked the most important question of all:

"At least tell us your name!"

Huginn's eyes, then, smiled.

"My name is Huginn. Goodbye, dear friends. May the gods assist you in this time of great and terrible events."

Then he took flight, hovering above the trees, where the sun broke through the clouds to kiss the world with its light. Beyond the valley, a stormy ocean of clouds completely blockaded its rays.

Huginn took courage; the unknown awaited him.

***

From that height his keen eye could sweep the entire landscape. There was the mountain range connected to the valley by a long rocky spine, from which he had fallen when the storm had knocked him down. Huginn realized that he would not have survived the fall from that height if the trees had not cushioned his fall.

What a bizarre sight it was, the view of the outside world compared to that of the valley: a barren and glacial landscape the first, a land full of life the second. These two worlds, so different from each other, coexisted within a few miles of each other, divided as they were by the mountains that encircled the valley.

The rock wall east of Hodmimir was the highest peak. Unlike its sisters, this mountain did not wear a green cloak of trees but was gray and barren. Huginn made a reconnaissance flight. He hoped, of course, to find his friend perched on a promontory, though after all the ups and downs he knew it would not be so easy.

Slightly below the summit was a large perfectly circular opening. The gallery did not seem natural, and Huginn thought it was most likely that giants had excavated it in a remote era of Midgard. His last experience in a cave warned Huginn of the dangers that could be hiding inside the mountain. Was it possible that Muninn, with all the trees to stop and rest among, would have preferred to take that dark tunnel? And did Muninn really take this path, or was the raven that the humans had seen just a common raven? Huginn was heartened at the thought that no other bird could have flown in such adverse weather conditions. Whatever had pushed Muninn to that mysterious valley, had also certainly led him into that tunnel. So, without lingering further, Huginn took courage and glided in to it.

The gallery was wider than it had appeared at first glance. It was high and spacious and its walls, circular in shape like the entrance, were perfectly smooth and regular. It was as if a giant worm had pierced the hard rock of the mountain. The passage continued straight for a while and then suddenly sloped downward into total darkness. Huginn longed to change into a bat, but it was a shame that even that spell of transformation, like most of his arcane repertory, was now forgotten. In any case he could not go forward in the dark, at the first turn of the passageway he would have crashed against the rock wall or worse. He then tried to remember anything that could be useful and finally, digging deep into his memory, he succeeded. He a squawked out a magic formula and was immediately surrounded by a dazzling silver light that in that sea of ink made him far too easy a target. Moreover, maintaining the spell did nothing but affect his energy reserves, weakening him and making escape more difficult.

The gallery wrapped upon itself, steep and winding like a coiled snake. Even the temperature, for some strange reason, suddenly dropped. On the way down, the light emanating from his magical aura revealed long veins of gold ore that shone along the passage with radiance; men, dwarves and giants would fight more than one war over this precious metal. Keeping the spell active, however, exhausted him and the walls of the gallery, so perfectly smooth, offered no ledge or outcropping for him to rest upon. If he stopped, he would probably fall to the heart of the world.

Finally, the gallery opened onto an ice cave so vast that he could not see its end. The cave was dimly lit by a bluish light of unknown origin that gave the place a ghostly glow. With his sharp eyesight, Huginn saw, more or less in the middle of the cave, the trunk of a colossal tree growing upwards. The tree was so big that it grew up to the roof of the cave, piercing the rock, pushing towards unknown peaks. Suddenly he had an illumination; what a fool he had been, not to remember! The Wood of Hodmimir was the top of the Tree of the World, Yggdrasill. Once, his Lord had told him how he had hung from its branches for days, trying to discover the secret runes … But to which of the three worlds did its roots belong to? Hel, Niflheim or Muspelheim?

The answer that Huginn sought came in the form of a roar whose echo shook the foundations of the world. At the foot of Yggdrasill, in fact, there was a dragon whose appearance and size had no equal in any of the nine worlds.

"And that, "Huginn reasoned, "must be the legendary Nidhogg, the dragon who has been gnawing at the roots of the World Tree since time began".

As further confirmation of his terrifying intuition, an ancient and evil voice thundered through the endless cave, shaking him from beak to claws.

"I SEE YOU! FOOL, YOU CANNOT HIDE!"

In an instant, Huginn was inundated by a gust of stale air that left him sick. Never in his millennia of existence had he felt as small and insignificant as at this time.

"I-I-" he tried to say, but his caw was lost in the void. Moreover, after having given his warning, the dragon became completely uninterested in him and returned to gnawing at the roots of the tree with renewed vigor. The root planted in Niflheim was about to break now. After a long eternity spent in that odious work, the dragon's patience would soon be rewarded with the ruinous fall of the tree.

Finding that the beast was no longer interested in him, Huginn took courage and, taking care to keep as far away as possible, landed on one of the mighty branches of the tree.

Not a minute had passed when, from above, he heard small steps approaching quickly in his direction. Looking up, Huginn saw a large, shaggy squirrel running in his direction.

"Out of the way, raven!"

Huginn had just enough time to move aside, thus preventing the squirrel from trampling him.

"Hey, wait! Stop a moment, I have to ask you something!"

Hearing that, the squirrel abruptly braked its crazy descent. He was running so fast that he just missed flying off the trunk.

"Hey! But you croak! That is, you speak! In fact, although I am a squirrel (the best and most beautiful of all squirrels!), I also speak and I also sing. By the way, would you like to hear a song?"

"Hmm… later, no doubt, with great pleasure. But first I wanted to ask you if by chance you may have seen a friend of mine …"

"A friend? What are you talking about? Here it's just me, old Nidhogg and that damned root that refuses to break. And so poor Ratatosk runs up and down the trunk of Yggdrasill for all eternity between the dragon and Widofnir[3] Mutually exchanging insults with the Golden Rooster — and just to add, those two are a little scarce in terms of imagination, especially old Nidhogg. And now, my dear speaking Raven, if you don't want to sing ♫I say goodbye! ♫".

"♪So / you haven't seen / another Raven like me? ♪".

"♫A Raven? / Why didn't you say so before / instead of wasting my time? /You will find no friends here / but of Ravens there is one, you know! / Right there, under the wing of the old one / it was caught / between the scapula and the rib / an exhausted hero / that for the dragon will become a hearty meal. / And now stand aside / no more can I delay / I have insults to deliver! ♫".

"♪Wait another second! /Help me free him /I will give you anything in exchange! ♪".

"Eh? Anything? Let me think about it, my dear raven. Hmm… why don't you give me a nice insult, something

---

[3] Variant for Víðópnir suggested by the scholar Karl Joseph Simrock.

that will send the old Niddhog on a rampage? A hundred years has past that he and the rooster do nothing but repeat the same things. You know, I think it's old age…"

Huginn understood that if he wanted to free Muninn he had no choice but to play the half-crazy squirrel's game. He thought about it for a while but no matter how hard he tried, he could not think of anything. Then, like a bolt out of the blue, he remembered an insult he had heard during his journey. His memory was getting better… Muninn had to be close by.

After hearing the insult from Huginn's beak, the squirrel's muzzle instantly wrinkled with heavenly joy.

"This will be a game changer!! This will be so amusing, you'll see!"

"You will keep your word? Help me free my friend?"

"Oh, I will do more…watch and learn, Raven!"

And this said, Ratatosk departed at a mad speed. Huginn could not conceive how the squirrel would even dare approach Niddhog, let alone insult him; the dragon terrified him! But for Ratatosk it seemed the simplest and most enjoyable thing in the world, and so Huginn, finding shelter in a crack of the big tree's trunk, hoped that the imminent gust of fire would not reach him, and began to observe…

Seeing the squirrel approaching, Nidhogg instantly stopped nibbling at the root. The serpentine pupil of its gigantic eye narrowed to a thin line. The squirrel refused to be intimidated and, on the contrary, allowed himself a derisive little smile that for any other creature would have meant incineration.

"I WAS WAITING FOR YOU, RATATOSK" said the dragon.

Without even answering him, the squirrel jumped onto his scaly head and snuck into his ear.

"As you get older you've become as impatient as a child, old snake. When was the last time you took a vacation? Must be at least a thousand years! And in exchange for what? Peanuts! Widofnir, however, he's a nice guy, always cheerful, always there to sing at dawn…"

The dragon snorted a cloud of sulphuric vapors, a clear sign that he was losing his patience and that it was better to cut it short.

"WHEN I HAVE FINISHED HERE, THAT BIRD WILL LOSE HIS BELOVED NEST! I WILL ROAST HIM WELL BEFORE EATING HIM" then he slicked his sharp bladelike teeth with his long forked tongue "BUT TELL ME, RATATOSK, WHAT DID HE TELL YOU THIS TIME? PERHAPS HE SAID THAT I SMELL LIKE A CADAVER? THAT I AM A WORM? COME ON, WHAT DID HE SAY?"

And, the question was asked, the same as it had been from the beginning of time, the dragon greedily awaiting the words of the impudent squirrel. Ratatosk took a deep breath before speaking. He knew that the old dragon's reaction this time would be terrifying.

"No, he said none of those things. Regarding your threat to toast him well before eating, the same threat you have used over the past 61 years, the great Widofnir says that … "if you take any more blood from your brain to digest his royal body, you'll end up becoming a complete idiot" Wanting to add something of his own, Ratatosk said "and he also says that it would not be noticed so much, since you have never shone with intelligence".

It took only a moment. The worm eyes of the Dragon filled with fire and the squirrel thought well of clinging with all his strength to the scales that encircled the ear of the beast to avoid being tossed away.

"ME, AN IDIOT?! RAAAURRR!"

The whole of Niflheim trembled, shaken by the tumult generated by the immense body of the raging dragon. On its broad, clawed wings, hung like gruesome trophies, were the skeletons of some of the bravest warriors in the history of Midgard. Over the millennia, those champions had attempted to cut down the dragon Nidhogg, thus meeting their end. The dream of returning triumphant to their people had become a horrible death and now, oblivious to the memory of men, they rotted among the scales, teeth and claws of the ancient dragon.

Huginn understood that if he wanted to free his friend he had to take advantage of that moment when the dragon was shaken and distracted with his outburst of anger. The raven, putting his own life at risk, moved as close as he could to the body of the colossus to scrutinize the innermost recesses of the dragon's skin. After a few minutes of scanning the immense body of the dragon, Huginn finally saw a black beak shining among the ribs of a warrior's skeleton. After all, Muninn must have noticed Huginn because at that precise moment he began to weakly move his wings, a signal that he was still alive.

Forgetting the danger, Huginn rushed to the rescue of his companion and, grasping him gently by the wings, proceeded to break the rib of the skeleton with strokes of his beak.

"Hold on, my friend!"

Then, using all the strength left to him, Huginn took flight, holding his friend firmly in his claws. Down below, completely unaware or indifferent to their fate, the dragon continued to vent its fury, producing clouds of fire and vapors from his wide and steaming nostrils.

Someone, however, had not forgotten them; as they fled on spread wings, Huginn heard a loud voice calling him: it was the squirrel Ratatosk, who had somehow managed to escape out of the dragon's ear and clung to the trunk of Yggdrasill.

"Ha ha ha! To die laughing for, right? Nidhogg will take a while to invent an insult of that caliber. And this, my dear raven, will delay the fall of Yggdrasill and the end of the world, at least for a few days! ♫Goodbye!♫".

***

During the long journey back home, Muninn was able to tell Huginn of all his misadventures. He told him first of how their Lord had ordered him to go to Niflheim to ascertain the conditions of the roots of the World Tree. The fall of Yggdrasill, in fact, was one of the signs of the advent of Ragnarök.

"Is it possible that you don't remember the Wood of Hodmimir, the top of the Tree of the Worlds?"

It was a rhetorical question: the one with the good memory had always been Muninn. Flying towards the Wood of Hodmimir, where the passage to Niflheim was located, Muninn had spotted entire columns of displaced people wandering aimlessly through the wasteland. Fearing their misfortune, he made a decision very similar to Huginn's when he had saved Lif and Lifthrasir from the berserkers: he had turned back more than once to show the humans the way to Hodmimir, thus going against their Lord's orders.

"But you should not have helped the worshipers of Loki find Hodmimir".

"You're wrong, Huginn, it was not me who guided the berserkers. They must have found another way in. Perhaps they tracked the humans, sniffing their trail, or maybe Loki guided them".

After attending to those unfortunates, Muninn had journeyed into the passage for Niflheim. At this point, a little annoyed by Muninn's fickleness, Huginn asked him if he had been afraid of the dragon.

"When I saw it, I was impressed, of course. But I remembered the many mortals who in the past had challenged Nidhogg and so, not to be outdone, I approached to ask him how much time he still needed to take down the Tree of the World. In response, the wretch tried to crush me with a wing but, as you already know, I was lucky enough to end up under the skeleton of someone not so lucky ..."

Muninn had a good memory but as far as common sense went he left a little to be desired. Yet Huginn was happy to be flying back home with his friend by his side.

Home, he finally saw her again, after that long and tiring journey. They had flown the blue depths of the sky, far beyond the clouds that enveloped the lands of Midgard, before seeing the abode of their Lord, the legendary palace of Valhalla. The palace could be accessed through 540 doors. Its walls were composed of the lances of the bravest warriors and the roof, shimmering in the morning sun, was made of gold shields depicting numerous war scenes. Usually, the palace swarmed with thousands of warriors, intent on practicing for combat or celebrating with a lavish banquet that never lacked music, beautiful Valkyries and rivers of beer and mead. It was therefore strange to find the building completely deserted. All the warriors had left on some secret mission in preparation for the Ragnarök, the last Great War that would proclaim the end of the universe.

The ravens wandered the long corridors in absolute silence. When, a little frightened, they entered the hall where usually boisterous banquets were held, that were legendary in all the Nine Worlds, Huginn and Muninn found their Lord sitting silently on his throne. The old god wore his magnificent armor, under whose weight he seemed to sink. His legendary weapon, the Gungnir spear, lay forgotten on the floor. Seeing them enter, the god shook his bearded head, apparently insecure about whether he was awake or dreaming.

"Great Odin" cawed Muninn, "we have returned."

The raven's words echoed in the hall relentlessly, like the tolling of a mourning bell. Perhaps the end had really come, for a moment later the god raised his venerable head.

"Huginn, Muninn…I have waited long for you…or so I remember. For days I could not think or remember anything… but now, everything is clear to me. Tell me, Muninn, how much time before the Tree falls?"

"Very little now, my Lord".

"I understand… courage, then, come to me".

He did not have to repeat himself; in a flash the two Ravens hopped onto his knees. Odin caressed them with the care of a grandfather for his grandchildren. His large, strong hands were capable of wielding any weapon, but when they wished, they also knew how to work in the fields and write poetry. In the distant past, when the Ravens were no more than chicks, those hands had taught them magical arts by weaving arcane symbols in the air. For this reason, Huginn and Muninn very much loved their Lord, whose power was matched by infinite wisdom and, if necessary, by instances of mercy.

Suddenly, two tears rained down on their heads. Odin was crying; he wept like a child imprisoned in the body of an old man, and those tears laboriously slipped through the immaculate curls of his long white beard like splinters of precious diamonds.

"Great Odin, why do you cry?" asked Huginn, whose heart ached immensely on seeing him suffer.

"Why?" he said to them, "I must say goodbye my dear friends. Know that I have always loved you."

And having said that, Odin got up and picked up the Gungnir spear from the ground. He set out from the palace, towards the barn, where, with a mighty cry that shook the foundations of Valhalla, he called to his noble eight-legged steed, Sleipner. The horse whinnied in return.

"Where do you now go, Great Odin?"

"Finally I remember, my friends, what my role in the final battle is." And mounting the horse, the god regained all of his past magnificence. "I go to Vígrídr, the plain where Surtr and the righteous gods will clash in the final battle. Do not wait for me, because I will not return…"

The noble Sleipner did not need commanding to leave at a gallop. In a few seconds, steed and horseman had already disappeared in the sea of clouds.

That's how Huginn and Muninn, *Thought* and *Memory*, watched the departure of their Lord. Odin would not survive the battle. His laughter, his voice and the sound of his steps would no longer echo in the halls of his dear home.

The small Ravens scanned the sky for a while. Then, after their Lord had disappeared into the horizon, they continued to watch, until the sky became fire and it was all over. So they watched, until *Thought* and *Memory* disappeared and the dream ended.

Contents

The Revolt of the Skeletons in the Closet

In the seemingly peaceful and pleasant town of Wolverhampton, England, an entrepreneur had the brilliant and terrifying idea of creating a Park of Horrors. The idea was the brainchild of Sir Desrius — better known as the "Warlock" — a cruel and unscrupulous man who did not hesitate to imprison monsters and fairy creatures from every corner of the globe to populate the park. For years now, the monsters have been forced to suffer abuse, yet for some time rumors have spread of a rebellion...

Dedicated to those who are victims of prejudice, "The Revolt of the Skeletons in the Closet" is a fairy tale that speaks straight to the heart of young and old alike.

The Final Reaping

A set of tarot cards that follows an enigma through the rooms of a dark and ghastly palace. A visionary tale of liberation.

"Stay alert. Surrender not to the Crows. Sing freely, and let your voice shake the foundations of the world."

The acclaimed graphic novel written by Jason R. Forbus and illustrated by Boris and Daria Sokolovsky now available in a refined hardcover edition.

www.ingramcontent.com/pod-product-compliance
Lightning Source LLC
Chambersburg PA
CBHW030403160726
47992CB00007B/2934